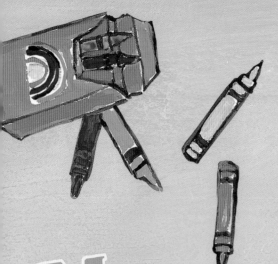

Moony Luna
Luna, Lunita Lunera

Story / Cuento
Jorge Argueta

Illustrations / Ilustraciones
Elizabeth Gómez

Children's Book Press, *an imprint of* Lee & Low Books Inc.
New York

Tomorrow
I'm going to school
for the very first time.
My heart skips just like a little frog.

My mommy Marisol shushes me,
"Calm down, moony little Luna!"

My daddy Luciano tickles me,
"It will be a great adventure,
Luna lunera!"

Mañana voy a la escuelita
por primera vez.
El corazón me salta
como una ranita.

Mi mami Marisol me dice:
—¡Cálmate, Luna, lunita lunera!

Mi papi Luciano me hace una cosquilla:
—¡Qué buena aventura te espera,
Luna lunera!

3

At bedtime, my mommy
reads me a story
about a little monster
who goes to school.

"That's how happy you'll be at school,"
my mommy Marisol tells me.

I listen to her soft voice
until I fall fast, fast asleep.

A la hora de dormir
mi mami me lee un cuento
de un monstruo pequeñito
que va a la escuela.

—¡Así vas a estar tú de alegre!
—me dice mi mami Marisol.

Escucho su voz suavecita
hasta que me quedo bien, bien dormida.

4

6

The next day . . .
"Wake up, moony Luna,
it's time to go to school,"
my mommy and daddy tell me.

I don't want to go to school!
Suppose there are monsters there,
ugly monsters with scary voices . . .

Al otro día...
—Despierta, Luna, lunita lunera.
Llegó la hora de ir a la escuela
—me dicen mi mami y mi papi.

¡No quiero ir a la escuela!
¿Qué pasa si allí hay monstruos,
monstruos feos de voces roncas?

I cover my head with my pillow
and start to cry
even though I'm five years old
and as big as the full moon.

"There's nothing to be afraid of."
My mommy puts her arms around me
and suddenly
I want to go to school.

Me tapo la cabeza con la almohada
y me pongo a llorar,
aunque ya tengo cinco años
y soy grande como la luna llena.

—No hay nada que temer.
—Mi mami me abraza
y de pronto me dan ganas
de ir a la escuela.

In the bathtub,
I think about the mean old voices
of the **monsters** who live at school.

I DON'T WANT TO GO TO SCHOOL!

En la tina, pienso en las voces roncas
de los **monstruos** de la escuela.

¡NO QUIERO IR A LA ESCUELA!

While my daddy combs my hair,
I think about the ugly faces
of the monsters who live at school.

I WANT TO STAY HOME!

Mientras mi papi me peina
pienso en las caras feas
de los monstruos de la escuela.

¡ME QUIERO QUEDAR EN CASA!

I'm five years old
and as big as the full moon
so I put on
my white socks,
my red sneakers,
my blue blouse,
and my green pants
all by myself.

And we head for school.

Como tengo cinco años
y soy grande como la luna llena,
me pongo
los calcetines blancos,
los tenis rojos,
la blusa azul
y unos pantalones verdes
yo solita.

Y nos vamos a la escuela.

In front of the school gate,
I yank on my mommy's hand
so that she'll stop RIGHT THERE.
"No, no," I tell her,
"I don't want to go to school!"
My mommy gives me a huge kiss.
I feel big and strong,
and, well, maybe I'll like school
just a little.

Frente al portón de la escuela,
le doy un tirón de la mano a mi mami
para que se pare ALLÍ MISMO.
—¡No! —le digo— ¡No!
Yo no quiero ir a la escuela.
Mi mami me da un beso grandote.
Me siento grande y fuerte.
Y, pues, quizás me guste la escuela
un poquitito.

A very nice teacher
says "hello" with a smile.
"Good morning, Lunita, and welcome!"

I hide behind my mommy's skirt.
I forget that I'm five years old
and as big as the full moon.

Room 105 ★ Salón 105

Una maestra simpatiquísima
nos saluda con una sonrisa.
—¡Buenos días, Lunita, y bienvenida!

Yo me escondo enseguida
detrás de la falda de mi mami.
Se me olvida que tengo cinco años
y soy grande como la luna llena.

My mommy says, "See you later."

Now there's no one here to call me
"Moony little Luna."

I run and hide under a table.
I'm going to stay here until
I'm six years old
and even bigger than the full moon.

Mami me dice: —Adiós y hasta pronto.

Ahora no hay quien me llame
« Luna, lunita lunera ».

Corro a meterme debajo de una mesa.
Aquí me voy a quedar
hasta que tenga seis años
y sea más grande que la luna llena.

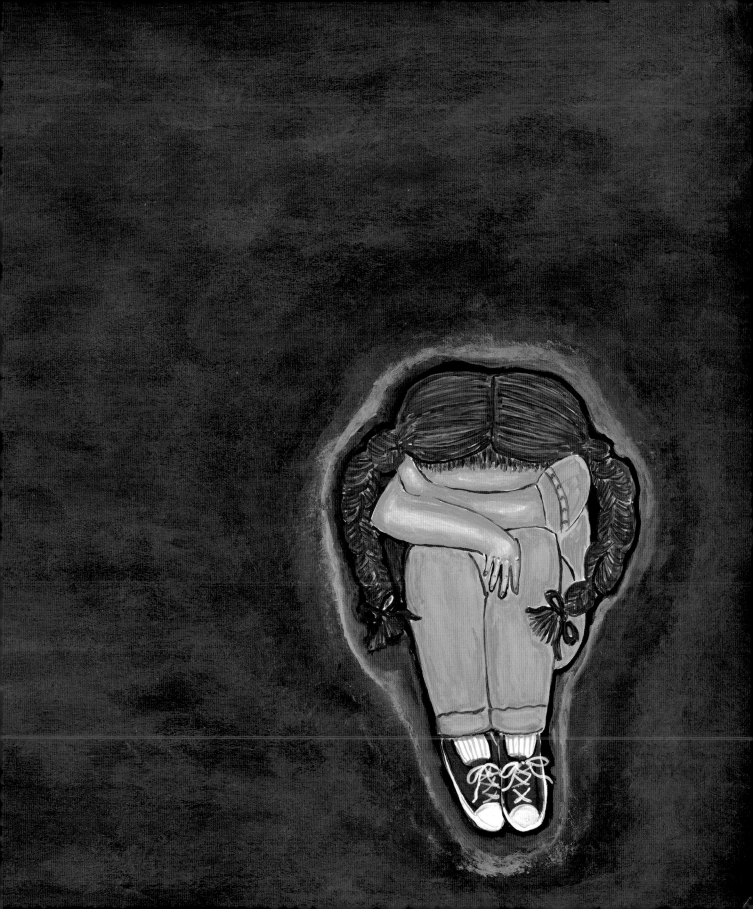

All of a sudden,
I see a little hand
here, under the table.
It wiggles five little fingers.

Then another hand, and another,
and another. Soon I see
lots of little hands under the table
and hear voices calling together,
"Moony Luna! Come out and play!"

22

De pronto, debajo de la mesa,
aparece una manita pequeña
con sus cinco deditos moviéndose.

Luego aparece otra, y otra,
y otra más hasta que debajo
de la mesa hay muchas manitas.
—Luna, lunita lunera —dicen
las niñas y los niños
que me invitan a jugar.

23

The children take my hand.
They bring me to the circle and they sing.

"Moony Luna, drink your milk
and go to school.
'Maybe I will and maybe I won't,'
croons the silly little moon."
Little by little, I start singing along with
Teresita, Mariita and Pablo José.

Los niños me toman de la mano.
Me llevan a la rueda y empiezan a cantar.

«Luna, lunita lunera,
bébete la leche y vete a la escuela.
Puede que sí, puede que no,
canta la luna, lunita lunera».

Poco a poco, comienzo a cantar
con Teresita, Mariita
y Pablo José.

Ms. Valentina
shows us the crayons and paper
she's set on our little tables.

I write my name in big letters:
LUNITA,
in bright colors—
red,
green,
and yellow.
Then I draw
the prettiest moon.

La maestra Valentina
nos lleva a unas mesitas
donde hay crayones y papel.

Yo escribo mi nombre en letras

grande:
LUNITA,
en colores—
rojo,
verde
y amarillo—
y dibujo una luna linda.

Afterwards Teresita, Mariita,
Pablo José, and I
line up like trains:
Tooooot! Tooot!
And then all of us sit in another circle.

Ms. Valentina reads us the story
of the nice little monster
who goes to school all by himself.

Después, Teresita, Mariita, Pablo José,
y yo hacemos fila como trencitos
—¡tuuuuuu, tuuuuuu!—
y hacemos otra ronda.

La maestra Valentina
nos lee el cuento
del monstruo muy bonito
que va a la escuelita él solito.

Before long,
my mommy Marisol and my daddy Luciano
come to pick me up at school.
I give them a little kiss and tell them
that no monsters live at my school.

And I whisper in their ears,
"You know, when I come back tomorrow,
I'll be even bigger than the full moon!"

Muy pronto mi mami Marisol
y mi papi Luciano
vienen a buscarme.
—En esta escuelita no viven
monstruos feos de voces roncas
—les explico, dándoles un besito.

Y les susurro en el oído:
—¿Saben? cuando vuelva mañana,
¡seré más grande que la luna llena!

Photo by Teresa Kennett

Jorge Argueta, a widely honored Salvadoran poet and writer, has a daughter Luna, who, when she was the age of the little girl in this story, had her own questions about school. Today he is the author of many children's books, including Children's Book Press' *A Movie in My Pillow* and *Xochitl and the Flowers*. These books have received numerous prizes, including the Américas Award, the Independent Publishers Award, and the Skipping Stones Honor Award.

Para Luna, que siempre será Lunita, y para Teresita. Ellas son la luna llena en mi córazon.
For Luna, who will always be Lunita, and for Teresita. They are the full moon in my heart.

—J. A.

Photo by Hernán Epelman

Elizabeth Gómez, a favorite of Children's Book Press readers for her brilliant illustrations for *The Upside Down Boy* and *A Movie in My Pillow*, is a native of Mexico City currently living in California. She has received high praise and numerous honors for her spirited, imaginative artwork, most currently, the América's Award—which is given at the Library of Congress—and the Latino Spirit Award. Her two daughters like having a painter for a mom, even if sometimes that means they have to be very quiet while she works.

Para nuestros niños: Bastián, Mijal, Carolina, Nicolás, Ana Lucía, Clara, Emiliano, Micaela, Isabel y Julián.
For our children: Bastián, Mijal, Carolina, Nicolás, Ana Lucía, Clara, Emiliano, Micaela, Isabel y Julián.

—E.G.

Para mi bebé: espero que este libro te dé fuerza en tu primer día de clases.
For my child: I hope this book will encourage you to be strong on the first day of school.

—**Lorena Piñon,** *Designer*

The illustrations were rendered in acrylic paints and crayons on rag paper
The text was set in the Ulissa and Berlin Myriad typeface family
The display was set in Farlowe Rough and Cafe Noir

Book design: Lorena Piñon, Pinwheel Productions
Book production: The Kids at Our House
Book editors: Ina Cumpiano, Dana Goldberg
Native reader: Laura Chastain

Library of Congress Cataloging-in-Publication Data
Argueta, Jorge.
Moony Luna / story, Jorge Argueta; illustrations, Elizabeth Gómez = Luna, Lunita Lunera / cuento, Jorge Argueta; ilustraciones, Elizabeth Gómez.
p. cm.
Summary: Five-year-old Luna is afraid she'll find monsters at her new school until a kind teacher and her new classmates show her that she has nothing to fear.
ISBN 978-0-89239-306-0 (paperback)
I. Title: Luna, Lunita Lunera. II. Gómez, Elizabeth. III. Title.
PZ73.A656 2005
2004056047

Manufactured in China by First Choice Printing Co. Ltd., January 2014
10 9 8 7 6 5 4 3 2 1
First Edition